KU-023-796

Contents

Horse-riding Hopes

Diana Gallagher

illustrated by Tuesday Mourning

www.raintreepublishers.co.uk
Visit our website to find out
more information about
Raintree books.

To order:
☎ Phone 0845 6044371
🖷 Fax +44 (0) 1865 312263
🖳 Email myorders@capstonepub.co.uk

Customers from outside the UK please telephone +44 1865 312262

Raintree is an imprint of Capstone Global Library Limited, a company incorporated in England and Wales having its registered office at 7 Pilgrim Street, London, EC4V 6LB – Registered company number: 6695582

"Raintree" is a registered trademark of Pearson Education Limited, under licence to Capstone Global Library Limited

Text © Stone Arch Books 2010
First published by Stone Arch Books in 2010
First published in hardback and paperback in the United Kingdom by
Capstone Global Library in 2010
The moral rights of the proprietor have been asserted.

Edited in the United Kingdom by Diyan Leake
Original illustrations © Stone Arch Books 2010
Illustrated by Tuesday Mourning
Originated by Capstone Global Library Ltd
Printed in China by Leo Paper Products Ltd

ISBN 978 1 406 21388 1 (hardback)
14 13 12 11 10
10 9 8 7 6 5 4 3 2 1

ISBN 978 1 406 21409 3 (paperback)
14 13 12 11 10
10 9 8 7 6 5 4 3 2 1

British Library Cataloguing in Publication Data
Gallagher, Diana – Horse-riding hopes
A full catalogue record for this book is available from the British Library.

Acknowledgements
We would like to thank the following for permission to reproduce photographs: Shutterstock Images/Close Encounters Photography cover (background)

Every effort has been made to contact copyright holders of material reproduced in this book. Any omissions will be rectified in subsequent printings if notice is given to the publisher.

Disclaimer
All the Internet addresses (URLs) given in this book were valid at the time of going to press. However, due to the dynamic nature of the Internet, some addresses may have changed, or sites may have changed or ceased to exist since publication. While the author and publisher regret any inconvenience this may cause readers, no responsibility for any such changes can be accepted by either the author or the publisher.

CHAPTER 1

New Stables

Molly Burke stopped walking and stared at the new flyer on the school notice board. "Pinch me, Kari," she said.

"Why?" her best friend asked.

"So that I know I'm not dreaming," Molly said. She rubbed her eyes and looked again.

She wasn't dreaming. The flyer said, "North Star Stables: Riding Lessons, Low Prices."

Kari looked at the flyer and sighed. "Oh," she said. "Riding lessons. I was hoping it was going to be something exciting."

"It *is* exciting!" Molly said.

Molly had loved horses since the first time she saw one on TV. She cut horse pictures out of magazines and saved them in a scrapbook. She had read all the horse books in the library, twice!

She collected glass horses and horse toys. The rocking-horse she had when she was little was still stored in the attic. But she'd never ridden on a real horse.

"This could totally change my life," Molly said.

"I thought your dad wouldn't let you take lessons," Kari said.

"He won't let me take lessons at Bay Meadow," Molly said. "Too expensive. But this says low prices!"

Kari leaned closer to read the small print on the flyer. "The instructor is a teacher in Year 6," she told Molly. "Her name is Miss North."

Molly smiled. "That will make it even easier to convince my parents to let me take lessons," she said. "Where are these new stables?"

Gabrielle and Lily walked up behind them. Molly spun around.

"What new stables?" Gabrielle asked, crossing her arms.

Molly looked at the flyer and read the address. "It says they're in Skylark Road," she said.

"I know that place. It's next to Bay Meadow," Lily said. "It's not new stables. It's an old farm." She and Gabrielle looked at each other and laughed.

Molly frowned. She knew that Gabrielle and Lily kept their horses at Bay Meadow. Sometimes they were allowed to wear riding clothes to school when they had horse shows, which Molly thought was really cool.

Molly had always wanted to be friends with Gabrielle and Lily, because they loved horses as much as she did. But Gabrielle and Lily didn't want to be friends with her. They only hung out with people who took lessons at Bay Meadow and owned horses of their own.

"I can't believe that somebody bought that old dump," Gabrielle added.

"Maybe Miss North has done it up," Kari said.

"Maybe, but I bet the horses are old and boring," Gabrielle said. "Riding school horses usually are. That's why Lily and I own our own horses. Having lessons at some old farm really isn't the same thing at all." She stuck her nose in the air. Then Gabrielle and Lily walked away.

Molly frowned. But she didn't care if it wasn't the same. She just wanted to learn how to ride a horse. As long as it had four legs, a mane, and a tail, any horse would be perfect.

Molly looked at the flyer. Then she wrote down the phone number in her notebook.

Dream Come True

At tea, Molly waited until her older
brother, Ken, had finished talking to their
parents about football practice. Then she
blurted out her news.

"A new riding-school stables just opened
on Skylark Road," Molly said quickly.
"The instructor is a Year Six teacher, and
it's cheaper than Bay Meadow. Can I take
riding lessons there?"

Her mum frowned. "That's a long way from here," Mum said. "You can't walk."

"I can ride my bike," Molly said. She cycled to school sometimes, and that was further away than the stables.

"I can drive her," Ken offered.

Molly smiled. Ken had just passed his driving test, and he'd do anything to drive the family car.

"Do you know the instructor's name?" her mum asked.

"Miss North," Molly said. "I wrote down the phone number."

Molly's mum and dad looked at each other.

"We'll think about it," her dad said finally. "Mum and I will talk after tea."

After tea, Molly went to her room to do her homework. She couldn't keep her mind on maths and history. All she could think about was horses. Molly wanted to learn to ride more than anything.

An hour later, there was a knock on Molly's bedroom door. Her mum walked in.

"Well, I talked to Miss North," Molly's mum said. She sat on the edge of Molly's bed and added, "She was very nice and answered all our questions."

"And?" Molly asked. She held her breath.

"Your dad and I decided that we will pay for ten group lessons," her mum said. "Miss North has a special rate for beginners, and she'll give us a refund if you don't like it."

"You must be joking!" Molly yelled happily. "I'll love it!"

Molly couldn't believe it. Her dream was coming true.

The only thing that would make it better would be if Kari would have lessons too. But Kari didn't like horses.

It didn't matter. Molly was finally going to learn how to ride.

CHAPTER 3

First Lesson

Molly had her first lesson a few days later. She had begged Kari to come and watch her first lesson, and Kari had finally given in. They rode their bikes to the stables together after school.

Molly had already changed into her new riding clothes. She was wearing long breeches and boots. The boots would make sure that her feet wouldn't slip through the stirrups while she was riding.

"This is it. Your big day," Kari said as they walked together towards the barn. "Are you excited?"

"Yes," Molly said with a nervous smile. "I'm so excited! I can't wait. My knees are shaking."

"Look at that!" Kari said, pointing to the field on the other side of the fence. A horse and rider galloped towards a tall hedge and jumped it.

"I wouldn't do that in a million years," Kari said. "Not even for a million pounds."

"I would!" Molly exclaimed. "I hope I can ride like that one day."

They walked inside the barn. Kari sat on a bench by the barn door, and Molly joined the other beginners. There were two girls and one boy.

A woman stepped forward. "You must be Molly Burke," she said. "I'm Miss North. Everyone is here now, so we can get started!"

Miss North led a big grey horse out of a stall and clipped two ropes to his halter. "Riding is only part of good horsemanship," she said. "Before you ride, you have to groom the horse."

Molly paid close attention as Miss North moved a rubber curry-comb in slow circles over the horse's neck, sides, and rump.

"Does he like that?" Molly asked. "It looks as if it might hurt."

Miss North laughed. "It doesn't hurt at all. Casper loves it," she said. "He loves it almost as much as he likes hay and oats. And he likes hay and oats a lot."

Miss North brushed the loose dirt off Casper. Then she used a cloth to make his coat shine. Finally, she combed Casper's mane and tail with a metal comb and untangled the snags with her fingers. Molly watched carefully.

"Who wants to clean his hooves?" Miss North asked. "Casper is old and lazy. He won't kick."

Molly was the only one who put her hand up. "I will," she said.

"Great, Molly," Miss North said. "Come over here and I'll show you what to do."

Molly did exactly what Miss North told her. When Molly touched the back of Casper's lower leg, he lifted his foot. Then she held his hoof and picked out the mud and stones with a metal hook tool.

"Very good, Molly!" Miss North said, smiling. "A horse with a stone in his hoof is like a car with a flat tyre. It can't go very far." The instructor put a saddle and bridle on Casper. "I'll teach you how to tack up a horse next time," she said.

"Doesn't 'tack' mean pinning something up?" the boy asked.

"Saddles and bridles are called tack, Max," Miss North explained. "Tacking up means putting them on the horse." She gave Casper's reins to Molly and said, "Take Casper to the arena."

Molly put one hand on the reins under Casper's chin and held the long ends of the reins in the other hand. She stayed on the left by his head. She had to tug on the reins and make a clucking noise to get Casper to move.

Kari hurried out of the barn ahead of them. "Horses seem like hard work to me," she said. "We've been here for half an hour, and you haven't even ridden one yet!"

"I think this part is fun too," Molly said, patting Casper's neck. "Hey, touch his nose," she told Molly. "It's so soft and warm."

Kari shuddered. "No way," she said.

The beginners led their horses into the ring and lined up in the middle. Miss North helped everyone to mount. As soon as Molly was on Casper, she grabbed the front of the saddle. It was a long way down!

"Remember," Miss North said, "horses are bigger, but people are cleverer. So never blame the horse when something goes wrong, even if it is his fault!"

Molly giggled. She was starting to feel more relaxed.

Miss North stood in the centre of the arena and explained the basics of good posture. "Sit up straight," she told the class. "Keep your elbows in and your heels down. To make the horse walk, tighten your reins and squeeze your legs."

Molly squeezed her legs, but Casper didn't move.

"Just kick gently him with your heel, Molly!" Miss North said.

Molly kicked, and the big horse started walking – straight towards the fence! Molly panicked. Was the horse going to keep walking and crash into the fence? It didn't seem like he was going to stop.

"What do I do?" she yelled.

"Pull back on the left rein," Miss North told her. "Don't pull out! Pull back!"

Molly pulled back on the rein in her left hand. Casper turned to the left and walked next to the fence. "Well done," Miss North called.

The other three horses were faster. Molly couldn't get Casper to speed up.

"You're all hunched up!" Kari said as Molly passed her. "And your reins are too loose."

When Molly shortened her reins and sat up straighter, Casper decided to catch up with the other horses. He broke into a slow trot, and Molly bounced up and down.

"Pull back on the reins to make him walk," Miss North said. "And keep those heels down, Molly."

Molly flopped around like a rag doll, but she got Casper to walk again. Then she heard someone laugh. She looked over the fence.

Gabrielle and Lily were riding in the Bay Meadow field. Their sleek horses pranced around, but both girls rode as if they were glued to their saddles. They slowed down and watched Molly for a moment. Then they giggled again.

Molly's cheeks flushed. She was really embarrassed, but she was determined to get it right. After all, Gabrielle and Lily had been beginners once. If they could learn to ride, so could she.

CHAPTER 4

Aches and Pains

The next morning, Molly woke up stiff and sore. Her muscles ached so much that it hurt to even brush her teeth. After she got dressed, she limped into the kitchen. Her family was already sitting at the table.

"What's wrong?" Mum asked. She poured Molly a glass of orange juice.

"My whole body hurts," Molly moaned.

"That's because riding uses muscles you haven't used before," her father said.

"No pain, no gain," Ken added. "That's what my football coach always says."

"My next lesson is in two days," Molly said. "How can I ride if I can hardly walk?"

"Have a hot bath after school," her mother suggested. "That might help."

"How did the riding go yesterday?" Dad asked.

"It wasn't what I expected," Molly said. "I thought I could just hop on and gallop off, but riding a horse is harder than it looks."

Her mother gasped. "Did the horse try to run away with you?" she asked nervously.

"No!" Molly said. She rolled her eyes and laughed. "The horse I rode only has two speeds. Slow and very slow."

"Good," Mum said, looking relieved. She paused. Then she said, "I know we've always said you've got to finish what you start, but we won't be annoyed if you want to stop riding."

"Stop riding? No way!" Molly exclaimed. She ached all over, and old Casper was slow, but Molly was already in love with riding!

* * *

On the way to school, Molly started worrying. She wanted to ask Kari to come with her to the next lesson, but Molly was pretty sure that Kari had been bored during the riding lesson.

What if Kari didn't want to go again? Molly knew that riding wouldn't be as much fun without her best friend.

Molly didn't say anything about it until they sat down for dinner. Then she asked Kari, "Are you busy on Saturday?"

"I don't think so," Kari said. "Why?"

"I really want you to come to my next lesson," Molly said. "It'll make me less nervous if you're there."

Just then, Gabrielle and Lily walked by with their dinner trays. They stopped and looked at Molly.

"You'll never learn to ride on that old horse you were riding yesterday," Lily said. "He's so old I bet he can't even stand up for ten minutes at a time."

Molly felt angry, but she didn't want Lily and Gabrielle to know. "Casper is quiet and calm," Molly told them. "That's why he's good for beginners."

"Young horses can get too excited sometimes," Kari said. "Sometimes they play up and buck or run away. Casper is a dependable horse."

Molly blinked. "When did Kari become a horse expert?" she wondered.

"Good point, Kari," Gabrielle said. "It'll be a long time before Molly can handle a horse like Rebel Wings."

Gabrielle's horse, Rebel Wings, was a junior show jumper. Show jumpers had to get over fences without knocking down rails. Points were taken off if a rail fell. Points were called faults, and a round with no faults was perfect. If more than one horse had zero faults, the fastest horse won.

Lily laughed. "There's no way Molly would ever be able to ride Jubilee," she said spitefully.

Lily's horse, Jubilee, was a junior working hunter. Working hunters had to get over the jumps and mind their manners. If a hunter bucked, it didn't win.

"We're riding in the Bay Meadows Junior Horse Show next week," Lily added.

"That sounds like fun," Molly said, "but you're right, Gabrielle. Rebel Wings is too nervous for me. I'm working really hard, though. I want to ride as well as you one day."

Molly could tell that the compliment surprised Gabrielle. Gabrielle just opened her mouth and then closed it again. Finally, she just mumbled, "Thanks."

Lily and Gabrielle walked away. Then Molly looked at Kari and asked, "When did you learn so much about horses?"

"I listened to everything Miss North told you," Kari said. "Riding is a lot more interesting than I thought it would be."

Molly grinned. "Does that mean you want to ride?" she asked.

"No!" Kari said loudly. She shook her head. "Absolutely not. But I *will* go to your lesson on Saturday."

"Great!" Molly said. But she was starting to realize something. Kari, who was usually not afraid of anything, was afraid of horses!

CHAPTER 5

Trail Trouble

Kari went to every lesson with Molly for two weeks. Kari watched the class ride, played with Miss North's dog, and petted the barn cat. But no matter what, she wouldn't ever touch a horse.

Molly liked having Kari's company at the stables, so she didn't tease her friend about being afraid of horses. Molly understood. After all, horses were really big! Molly loved them, but Kari didn't have to.

"I offered to feed the horses and do some other jobs at North Star today," Molly told Kari one Monday. "Kids who help out get extra riding time. Miss North has parent–teacher meetings after school. Do you want to help?"

"Okay," Kari said, "but I'm not going anywhere near the horses' stalls."

"You won't have to," Molly said. "Promise."

After school, Ken drove Molly and Kari to the stables. When Molly walked into the barn, she felt really nervous. Even though Miss North had shown Molly what to do, she was nervous about doing the jobs on her own. She didn't want to make a mess of them.

"Where do we start?" Kari asked. She followed Molly into the tack room.

Rows of saddle and bridle racks covered the walls. Three dirty bridles hung down from a hook on the ceiling.

Molly pointed at the bridles. "Let's clean tack," she said.

"I'll get the hot water," Kari said.

Kari filled a bucket at the sink and set it down. Molly unhooked the bridles. Then Kari washed dried grass off the metal bits. When she finished cleaning the bits, she put the bridles back on the hook.

Molly rubbed a bar of orange saddle soap with a wet sponge and cleaned the leather straps. After she rinsed off the soap with another sponge, Kari dried the straps with a cloth and rubbed in leather conditioner. Finally, they hung the clean bridles on the wall.

Kari dumped the dirty water in the sink and put the bucket away. "I don't know why," she said, "but I don't mind cleaning here. Even though I hate it at home."

"I know," Molly said. "I feel the same way. I hate cleaning at home too, but here, it's sort of fun!"

Kari smiled. "Now what?" she asked.

"I'll get the hay, and you fill the water buckets," Molly said.

"Sounds good," Kari said, smiling. She pulled a hose over to Casper's stall. Standing outside the stall, she stuck the hose through the bars into his bucket and filled it up.

Molly headed outside to the hay bales. She wasn't strong enough to drag a whole bale of hay into the barn.

Instead, Molly peeled off sections and put them in a wheelbarrow. Then she carted the hay inside.

The horses didn't try to leave when Molly opened the stall doors. They knew it was time for dinner. She tossed a large clump into the corner of every stall.

"Do we have to feed them anything else?" Kari asked.

"No," Molly told her. "Miss North said she'd give them the rest of their food when she gets home."

"So what's next?" Kari asked.

"We have to muck out," Molly said. "You know, get the dirty straw out of the stalls."

"I don't want to muck out," Kari said. "I'll sweep."

"That's fine," Molly said.

She used a pitchfork and a huge plastic bucket to take wet straw and manure out of every stall. Miss North cleaned the stalls really well every morning, so there wasn't much.

Kari stood back to admire her work. She had swept every bit of hay and dirt off the floor. "Is that it?" she asked.

"Just about," Molly said. She quickly checked the stall doors to make sure they were latched. "All done," she said.

The two girls walked outside and sat on the fence to wait for Ken to pick them up. A few minutes later, Gabrielle rode by on Rebel Wings.

"Hi, Gabrielle," Molly said. "Where's Lily?"

"She's at the dentist," Gabrielle said. "Will you open that gate for me?"

Molly opened the gate to the bridle paths. Gabrielle rode through. As the horse and rider turned towards the woods, Molly frowned. She called out, "It's not safe to ride down there on your own!"

Gabrielle didn't look back. She trotted Rebel Wings down the bridle path and disappeared into the trees.

"I'm sure she'll be fine," Kari said. But Molly wasn't so sure. And a few minutes later, they heard Gabrielle scream.

Risky Rescue

"Something's wrong," Molly said.

"I'll go and call Miss North," Kari said. She headed for the barn. "I saw a phone in the tack room."

"Miss North is too far away," Molly said, running ahead. "I'm going to get Casper and go and find Gabrielle." She opened the barn door and went inside.

"You can't take a horse out alone!" Kari exclaimed.

"I know, but this is an emergency," Molly said. She took a deep breath and looked Kari in the eye. "You'll have to hold Casper while I get on."

Kari gasped. "No way," she said.

"Kari, you have to," Molly said. "I need your help. And so does Gabrielle."

"But what if he bites me?" Kari asked nervously. "Or kicks me? Or steps on my foot or something? I really can't touch that horse."

"He won't do anything," Molly said. "Come on. If Gabrielle is hurt, we've got to help her."

Kari took a deep breath. "Okay," she said. She got Casper's saddle and bridle from the tack room. Then she stood back as Molly took Casper out of his stall.

Molly had to hurry, so she only had time to quickly brush the horse's back and check his feet for stones. After she put Casper's saddle on, she led him outside. Kari slowly followed.

"This isn't hard, Kari," Molly said. "Just hold the reins tight under his chin so he can't walk away."

Kari slowly walked up to the horse. Her hand shook when she took the reins. Molly knew that would make some horses nervous, but Casper didn't even twitch.

"What if he moves?" Kari asked.

"Pull back and say, 'Whoa!'," Molly told her.

Molly stretched to get her left foot in the stirrup. Then she grabbed the saddle, hopped, and pulled herself up.

"Okay. I'm on," she said.

Kari gave Casper a quick pat on the neck and stepped back. "Good luck," she told Molly.

Molly turned Casper down the bridle path and kicked him into a trot.

The trail through the woods was pretty, but Molly was too worried about Gabrielle to enjoy it. After a few minutes, she pulled Casper back to a slow trot. She didn't want to move too quickly, in case she had to duck under a tree branch.

"Gabrielle!" Molly yelled. "Gabrielle!"

"I'm over here!" Gabrielle called.

Molly trotted Casper forwards. Soon, she spotted Gabrielle sitting on a big log.

"What happened?" Molly asked.

Gabrielle stood up and brushed off her breeches. She had mud on her face, but she didn't look hurt. "A stupid squirrel scared Rebel," she said. "He moved back, and I fell off."

"Where is Rebel?" Molly asked.

"He ran away," Gabrielle said. "I tried to catch him, but he's too fast. I'm really worried."

"Casper's not very speedy, but he goes faster than we can," Molly told her. She moved the horse over to the log and said, "Get on behind me."

Gabrielle frowned and asked, "Are you sure he rides double? If he can only handle one rider, this is a really bad idea."

"It's fine," Molly said. "Nothing bothers Casper."

After Gabrielle got on, Molly kicked Casper into a slow jog. Both girls searched the woods for the lost horse.

After a few minutes, Gabrielle gasped. "There he is!" she said, pointing ahead.

Rebel's reins were tangled in a patch of bushes. He was breathing hard, and sweat covered his coat. He was stuck, scared, and tired.

Gabrielle slid to the ground. She moved slowly towards Rebel, talking softly as she walked.

"Easy, boy. It's okay," she said quietly. She untangled the reins and led Rebel out of the brush. Then she carefully got on his back.

"Are you sure you're okay?" Molly asked.

"Yeah. Thanks," Gabrielle said. She turned and rode back towards the barn.

Molly frowned. Then she patted Casper's neck. "Good boy," she said softly. "You saved the day."

CHAPTER 7

Horse Show

A few weeks later, Molly grinned as she looked out over the Bay Meadow Junior Horse Show.

Jeeps and horse trailers were parked in one field. Red, white, and blue jumps were set up in the large show arena. Young riders were brushing horses or riding in the practice ring. They all wore hard hats, breeches, and shiny boots. Some were also wearing hunting coats and shirts with wide cravats.

"I can't believe we're here!" Molly exclaimed.

"It would be more fun if you were riding," Kari said.

"Yeah, but there's an entry fee for every class," Molly explained. "I didn't want to ask my parents for more money. We'll still have fun helping the others."

Four other people from Miss North's class were riding in beginner groups. Molly and Kari had come to watch, work, and learn.

Miss North walked Casper down the ramp of her horse trailer.

"Kari, can you hold Casper for a few minutes?" Miss North asked. "It's all right to let him eat grass."

"Sure," Kari said. She took the lead rope and led Casper to a patch of green grass.

Molly smiled. Kari still didn't want to ride, but she liked taking care of the gentle old horse.

"Molly, will you take these entry forms and fees to the show tent?" Miss North asked. She pointed towards the arena. "They'll give you number cards for our riders."

"Sure," Molly said. "I'll be right back!"

She hurried to the tent. After she handed in the forms, she wrote each rider's name on a number card. Every rider would wear a different number.

While the people from Miss North's class practised, Molly and Kari watched the other riders. In the first group, the riders were asked to walk, trot, and canter. The judge scored the riders on how well they rode.

In groups like Gabrielle's junior jumper group and Lily's hunter group, the judge scored the horses, not the riders.

Molly and Kari watched as Gabrielle entered the ring and eased her horse into a canter. Then it was time for the jumps. The jumps were made of rails, white gates, and bushes.

Rebel Wings cleared every jump without knocking anything down. Molly clapped and cheered when he won a red rosette for first place.

In the hunter group, Lily's horse cleared every fence, but hunters were also judged on looks, gait, and manners. Jubilee won a yellow rosette for third place.

"We'd better get back," Kari said. "I promised to help Max get Casper ready."

When they got back to the trailer, Max was sitting on the ramp. He didn't look very happy.

"What's wrong, Max?" Molly asked.

"I don't want to compete," Max said. "I bounce around too much. It's really embarrassing."

"It's all right, Max," Miss North said, smiling. "Horse shows should be fun. You don't have to ride if you don't want to."

"Molly knows how to walk and trot," Kari said. "She could compete instead."

"Yeah, let Molly ride!" Max said. "Then it's not a waste of my entry fee. That will make my mum happy."

"I can't be in the show!" Molly exclaimed. "I didn't bring my riding clothes."

"You're right. That is a problem," Miss North said. "I have an extra hard hat, but you need breeches and boots."

"Could we borrow some?" Kari asked.

Molly looked at the other North Star kids. They were all younger, and their clothes were too small. She really wanted to ride, but she couldn't do it without the right clothes. The horse show had strict rules.

"Don't give up," Miss North said. "Tack Casper up, and I'll check with the other teachers. Someone must have clothes in your size that we can use."

Molly and Kari each brushed one side of the horse. Kari combed out his mane and tail, and Molly polished his hooves with oil to make them shine. Then they put on his saddle and bridle.

Soon, Miss North was back, frowning. "Sorry, Molly. No luck," she said.

Molly put down the brush she'd been using to smooth Casper's coat. "Thanks for trying," she said. She smiled, but she felt really disappointed.

Then she heard a shout. "Molly!"

Molly looked up. Gabrielle and Lily were running towards her. "I heard you had a problem," Gabrielle said.

Molly nodded. "I can't ride in the walk-trot class because I didn't bring my riding gear," she explained.

"We always bring an extra set of clothes," Lily said.

"In case we fall in the mud or it rains," Gabrielle said. "You can borrow my clothes," she added. "They should fit you."

"Really?" Molly said.

Gabrielle shrugged and smiled. "I owe you a favour," she said. She handed a bundle of clothes to Molly.

Kari looked at her watch. "You've only got ten minutes!" she said. "Go and change, Molly. I'll take Casper to the arena!"

CHAPTER 8

The Great Casper

Miss North pinned a number card to the back of Molly's coat. Then she gave her a boost on to Casper's back.

Molly was nervous. "I don't want to mess it up," she admitted.

"You'll be fine," Miss North said. "Casper knows what to do."

Molly looked over to the fence nearby, where her teammates were watching. Lily and Gabrielle were there too.

"Good luck," Lily said. She gave Molly a thumbs-up.

"I hope you win a rosette," Gabrielle said.

"Did you win a ribbon in your first horse show?" Kari asked.

"Yep," Gabrielle said. She grinned. "I came in sixth. Out of six."

Molly counted the horses waiting at the gate. Twelve. Six rosettes would be awarded, so she had a fifty-fifty chance. Winning would be nice, but she was just glad to be riding in the show.

As the other riders moved into the ring, Miss North gave Molly some advice. "Stay close to the fence," Miss North said. "Don't get bunched up with the other horses."

"Okay," Molly said.

She shortened her reins, sat up straight, and entered the arena. The minute the gate closed, Casper's ears perked up. He walked a little faster and picked up his feet. Molly smiled. She knew that Casper was showing off for the judges.

"Walk!" the announcer said over the loudspeakers.

Miss North stood by the fence. "You're looking good, Molly!" she called. "Push those heels down."

Molly pushed her heels down and looked straight ahead.

"Trot!" the announcer said. Casper started trotting.

Kari was standing on the opposite side of the big show ring. As Molly rode by, Kari yelled, "Elbows in!"

Molly tucked in her elbows. There was so much to remember. She was glad to have a second instructor.

"Walk," the announcer said, "and reverse."

Molly turned Casper towards the centre of the ring and changed directions. She smiled.

Then she realized that she'd stopped being nervous. In fact, she'd started enjoying herself.

The announcer ran through the same set of instructions again. When the group trotted, two horses rushed up behind Casper. They passed too close, startling Molly. She tensed, but Casper kept going as if nothing had happened.

"Walk!" the announcer called.

That was it. It was over.

Kari smiled when Molly and Casper walked by. "You were fantastic!" she said.

"Thanks for the help," Molly said. "It was fun. You should try riding sometime."

"Maybe I will," Kari said. "Miss North said that you're good enough to ride Rainbow now, so maybe I can try riding Casper."

Molly was thrilled. Things couldn't get much better. Rainbow was Miss North's best horse, and Kari wanted to ride!

"Line up, please," the announcer said.

Molly rode into the centre of the arena. The riders lined up side by side. The judge walked behind them and wrote the winning numbers on his clipboard. Then he handed the clipboard to the announcer.

A few horses jiggled while they waited. Casper stood still, and Molly patted him on the neck. He was the perfect horse for her first show. She knew she wouldn't win, but she'd had a great time.

The announcer called out first and second place. The riders rode up to the judge, who handed them blue and red rosettes. Then the announcer said, "Third place goes to Molly Burke on Casper."

Molly's jaw dropped. "What?" she said. Then she heard cheering coming from her friends near the fence.

Molly smiled. Then she rode Casper over to the judge and accepted her first rosette.

ABOUT THE AUTHOR

Diana Gallagher lives with her husband and five dogs, four cats, and a stroppy parrot. She has been an English equitation instructor, a professional folk musician, and an artist. However, she had aspirations to be a professional writer at the age of twelve. She has written dozens of books for children and young adults.

ABOUT THE ILLUSTRATOR

When Tuesday Mourning was a little girl, she knew she wanted to be an artist when she grew up. Now, she is an illustrator who is especially keen on working on books for children and teenagers. When she isn't illustrating, Tuesday loves spending time with her husband, who is an actor, and their son, Atticus.

GLOSSARY

breeches knee-length trousers that are tight at the bottom

canter motion a horse makes when it runs at speed between a trot and a gallop

curry-comb special brush used for cleaning horses

dependable reliable

emergency dangerous situation that must be handled right away

gait way of walking

gallop motion a horse makes when it runs as fast as it can

groom brush and clean a horse

reins straps that help control a horse

stables place where horses are kept

stirrup loop that hangs down from a saddle, where a rider's foot goes

trot motion a horse makes when it moves quickly but more slowly than when it canters

MORE ABOUT HORSE RIDING

Learning how to ride a horse takes time. It also takes proper training. However, it does not take much equipment. You don't need your own horse, and you certainly don't need fancy clothes.

A beginner rider will need:

- a pair of sturdy boots with a low heel

- comfortable trousers

- good gloves

- a riding helmet

The horse, saddle, and other equipment should be available at the stables.

The best place to learn to ride is at a riding school. Look for a school that has clean stables and healthy horses. Also make sure that the school has qualified instructors and small class sizes.

At a riding school, you will learn how to properly groom and ride a horse. To find a good riding school in your area, check with The Pony Club. (You can search online for The Pony Club, or ask a parent or teacher for help.)

It takes time to build a relationship with a horse. You must be patient. With training and time, a horse can become a great friend.

DISCUSSION QUESTIONS

1. Why were Gabrielle and Lily unkind to Molly at the beginning of this book? Do you think Molly handled it correctly?

2. In chapter 6, Molly takes a risk when she rides into the woods alone to help Gabrielle. Do you think she did the right thing? Why or why not? What else could she have done to help Gabrielle?

3. Do you know any other books, stories, films, or TV programmes about riding? Talk about other things you know about horse riding.

WRITING PROMPTS

1. Molly has always wanted to be able to take riding lessons. Write about something you have always wanted to do.

2. Molly's best friend, Kari, goes to Molly's riding lessons even though Kari isn't interested in riding. Write about a time when you did something your best friend wanted to do, even though you weren't interested.

3. At the end of this book, Molly wins a rosette. Write about a time that you won something. What did you do? What did you win?

FIND OUT MORE

Books

Chestnut Hill series, Lauren Brooke (Scholastic, 2009)

Complete Book of Riding and Pony Care, Gill Harvey and Rosie Dickins (Usborne, 2009)

Horse (Eyewonder series, Dorling Kindersley, 2010)

Horse and Pony Handbook, Camilla La Bedoyere (Miles Kelly, 2009)

Pony Club Secrets series, Stacy Gregg (HarperCollins, 2009)

Pony Whisperer series, Janet Rising (Puffin, 2009)

Website

http://www.horseridinglesson.co.uk/
This website has tips and advice on learning to ride.